Pinwheel Days

By Ellen Tarlow

Art by Gretel Parker

D0483227

Star Bright Books
New York

Published in the United States of America by Star Bright Books, Inc., New York.
The name Star Bright Books and the Star Bright Books logo are registered
trademarks of Star Bright Books, Inc. Please visit www.starbrightbooks.com.

ISBN-13: 978-1-59572-059-7
ISBN-10: 1-59572-059-6

Printed in India (NU) 9 8 7 6 5 4 3 2 1

Library of Congress Cataloging-in-Publication Data

Tarlow, Ellen.
 Pinwheel days / by Ellen Tarlow ; illustrated by Gretel Parker.
   p. cm.
 Summary: In four separate stories, Pinwheel the donkey learns about friendship
when his loneliness ends after meeting his "echo," a lovely picnic stems from a
mistake, his rubbing on a tree seems to break it, and his best dream ever comes true.
 ISBN-13: 978-1-59572-059-7 (pbk.)
 ISBN-10: 1-59572-059-6 (pbk.)
 [1. Friendship--Fiction. 2. Donkeys--Fiction. 3. Forest animals--Fiction.]
I. Parker, Gretel, ill. II. Title.

PZ7.T174Pin 2006
[E]--dc22
                                        2006021030

Contents

The Echo

Pinwheel the donkey was busy kicking.

He kicked with his right foot.

"Pow!" he said.

He kicked with his left foot.

"Bam!" he said.

Then he stopped.

"I wish I had someone to play with," he said.

"I wish I had someone to play with," came a voice.

Pinwheel turned.

But no one was there.

"I want to play hide-and-seek,"
said Pinwheel.
"I want to play hide-and-seek,"
said the voice.

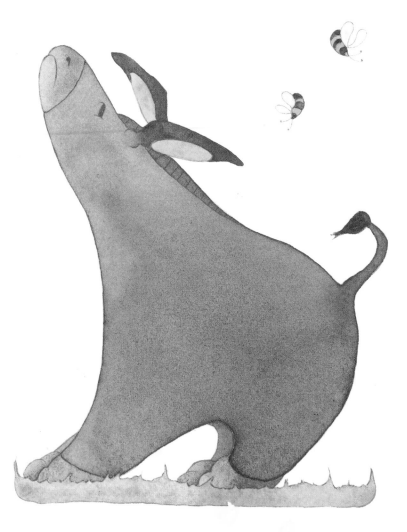

"I like peanut butter for lunch,"
said Pinwheel.

"I like peanut butter for lunch,"
said the voice.

Pinwheel smiled. He had an echo!

"I like to look for rocks after lunch,"
he said to the echo.

"I like to climb trees after lunch,"
the echo said back.

"No, I don't!" cried Pinwheel. "I like
to look for rocks."

"You don't ever like to climb trees?"
asked the echo.
"Echo!" said Pinwheel. "You are
supposed to listen to me.
Then you can talk."
The echo laughed.
Pinwheel laughed. Then he stopped.
"Echo," he said. "I am supposed to
laugh first. Then you can laugh."

"But I am not an echo," said the echo.

"Look up here."

Pinwheel looked up.

He saw a squirrel.

"Hello," said the squirrel.

"I am Squirrel."

Pinwheel felt silly.

His echo was a squirrel!

"I am Pinwheel," said Pinwheel.

"Do you want to play hide-and-seek?" asked Squirrel. "You can be It."

"I will close my eyes and count to ten," said Pinwheel.

Squirrel hid in a log.

But Pinwheel found him.

Pinwheel hid behind a bush.

But Squirrel found him.

Soon it was time for lunch.
Pinwheel went to his house.
He made his best peanut butter
sandwich.
"I will give this to Squirrel," he said.
"He can have peanut butter for
lunch. He likes that."

Pinwheel heard a knock.

It was Squirrel.

"Hello, Pinwheel. I brought you a
peanut butter sandwich for lunch,"
said Squirrel.

"But Squirrel," said Pinwheel. "I was going to bring <u>you</u> a peanut butter sandwich for lunch."

Pinwheel gave Squirrel his sandwich. Squirrel took a bite.

Squirrel gave Pinwheel his sandwich. Pinwheel took a bite.

"This is the best peanut butter sandwich I ever had!" said Squirrel.

"This is the best peanut butter sandwich I ever had!" said Pinwheel.

"Echo!" they both said.

They laughed.

Then they ate their sandwiches together.

Waving

Pinwheel and Squirrel were going to go sailing.

Squirrel was at the pond.

He was waving.

"Hello, Squirrel!" Pinwheel called.

He waved to Squirrel.

"I'm not waving at you, Pinwheel," said Squirrel. "Look out there."

Pinwheel looked across the pond.

He saw something moving.

"See?" asked Squirrel. "I don't know who it is, but they keep waving."

"They must be very friendly,"
said Pinwheel.

"Too friendly," said Squirrel.

"My arm hurts."

"Let me wave," said Pinwheel.

"I wonder who it is," said Squirrel.

"Who are you?" Pinwheel called.

But no one answered.

He waved harder.

"Maybe they will get tired soon,"
said Pinwheel.

Squirrel looked out.

"I don't think so," he said.

Pinwheel and Squirrel waved together.

"I'm coming," a voice called.

It was Rabbit.

She was waving.

"Hello, Rabbit," they said.

"We are not waving at you."

"You are not?" asked Rabbit.

"No," said Squirrel.

"Look out there."

"Who is it?" asked Rabbit.

"We don't know," said Pinwheel.

"But they keep waving."

"How friendly," said Rabbit.

Pinwheel rubbed his arm.

"Can you wave now?" he asked Rabbit.

"Gladly," said Rabbit.

She started to wave.

Then she stopped.

She rubbed her arm.

Pinwheel waved.

He waved and waved.

He rubbed his arm.

"This is making me hungry," he said.

"Oh, yes," said Rabbit.

"Let's have lunch," said Squirrel.

He took out his sandwich.

Pinwheel took out his sandwich.

Rabbit looked at them.

"Can you wave while we eat?"
asked Pinwheel.

"I don't think so," said Rabbit.

"I am very hungry and my arm hurts."

They all looked out across the pond.

Pinwheel had an idea.

"Let's sail to the other side of the pond," he said.

"Then we can see who is waving."

They all got into the little boat.

Pinwheel held onto the tiller and steered the boat.

Squirrel worked the sail.

Rabbit watched the food.

Soon they were at the other side.

"Hello-oo!" they called.

But no one answered.

They looked this way and that way.

They looked all around.

But all they could see was

a tall white flower.

"Maybe they are shy," said Squirrel.

"Maybe they went to find us,"
said Pinwheel.

They set out their picnic.

The wind blew.

The tall white flower
moved from side to side.

"I think I have seen that before,"
said Rabbit.

"Me too," said Pinwheel.

"Me too," said Squirrel.

Squirrel waved at the flower.

Then Pinwheel waved.

Then Rabbit waved.

They laughed.

"Well, it is a very nice place for a picnic," said Squirrel.

"Let's all eat," said Pinwheel.

"Thank you for inviting me," said
Rabbit.

"Thank you for coming," said Squirrel.

"Thank you for inviting us,"
Pinwheel said to the flower.

The wind blew.

The flower nodded.

Happy Fall!

Pinwheel was waiting for Squirrel.

"I like Squirrel and Squirrel likes me,"

he sang.

"Pinwheel! Be quiet!" said a voice.

"I am trying to sleep."

It was Owl.

"I am sorry, Owl," said Pinwheel.

Pinwheel felt an itch.

He rubbed against the tree.

"Pinwheel!" shouted Owl.

"Stop bumping the tree!

My bed is shaking."

"I am sorry, Owl," said Pinwheel.

Pinwheel stood as still as he could.

Something soft touched his head.

"What is that?" he wondered.

He shook his head. A red leaf fell.

The wind blew. More leaves fell.

"1, 2, 3, 4, 5," Pinwheel counted.

"Oh, no!" he said. "I broke the tree."

"Hello, Pinwheel," said Squirrel.

"Squirrel, I broke the tree!"
cried Pinwheel.

"Owl is going to be so mad at me!"

"Are you sure it's broken?"
asked Squirrel.

The wind blew. More leaves fell.

"6, 7, 8, 9, 10," Pinwheel counted.

"See?" he said. "Broken."

"Very broken," said Squirrel.

They looked up. More leaves fell.

"Go back!" they shouted.

But the leaves kept on falling.

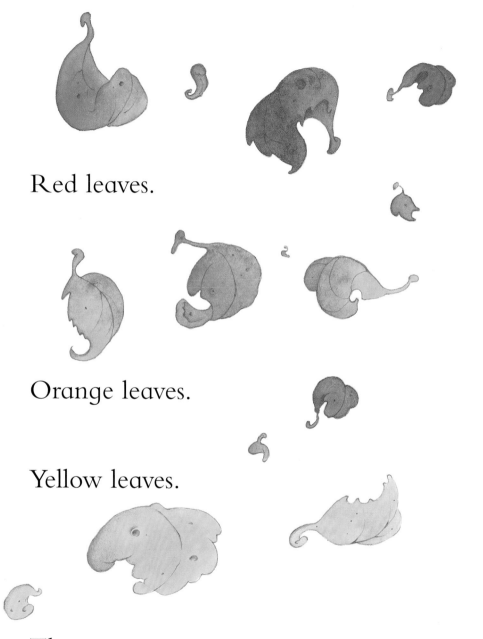

Red leaves.

Orange leaves.

Yellow leaves.

There were too many to count.

"You won't like it down here,"
Pinwheel told the leaves.
"You will only get stepped on,"
said Squirrel.
"And squashed," added Pinwheel.
"Very squashed," said Squirrel.
"Let's show them," said Pinwheel.
"Good thinking," said Squirrel.
He climbed up the tree trunk.
"Look out below!" he shouted.
He jumped into a pile of leaves.
"See?" Pinwheel told the leaves.
"Squashed!"
Then he heard laughing.
"Pinwheel," laughed Squirrel.
"Jump in!"

Squirrel popped out of the leaves.

He jumped back in.

Then Pinwheel jumped in.

"Catch me!" called Squirrel.

"Be quiet, you two!" said a voice.

Owl stepped out of his house.

He looked around. "Ah, fall!" he said.

He looked down.

"Hide!" said Squirrel.

"Where?" asked Pinwheel.

"Look out below!" shouted Owl.

He jumped into the leaves.

"Run!" said Squirrel.

But it was too late.

"Hello," said Owl. "Happy fall!"

"Fall?" asked Pinwheel.

"Fall?" asked Squirrel.

"It's my favorite season," said Owl.
Pinwheel looked at the colorful
leaves.
"Happy fall!" he shouted as loudly as
he could.
Then he jumped in to find Squirrel.

Pinwheel's Dream

It was morning.

Pinwheel opened his eyes.

He was smiling.

In his dream, he had been flying.

"Where was I flying to?" he wondered.

"What was I going to do?"

Pinwheel sighed.

Now he would never know.

Then he had an idea.

"Today I will stay in bed," he said.

"I will try to dream something wonderful."

He fluffed his pillow.

He pulled up the covers.

He closed his eyes.

"Dream, I am ready," he whispered.

"Pinwheel!" called Squirrel.

"I am hiding. Come and find me!"

Pinwheel got out of bed.

"I cannot play hide-and-seek," he called back. "I am going to have my best dream ever."

"But Pinwheel," called Squirrel.
"This is my best hiding place ever!
Who will find me?"
Pinwheel went back to bed.
"Dream, come and find me," he
whispered.

Pinwheel smelled something good.

"Pinwheel, get up!" said Rabbit.

"I made muffins. When they are cool,
we can eat them."

"Rabbit," said Pinwheel.

"I have no time for muffins.
I am too busy sleeping.
I am trying to have my best
dream ever."

"Is it night again?" asked Rabbit.
"It seems like it was just morning."
Pinwheel pulled the covers up.
"Dream, now I am really, really
ready," he whispered.

Pinwheel heard a flapping sound.

It was Owl.

"Wake up, Pinwheel!" said Owl.

"The sun is out.

The flowers are blooming.

There are colors everywhere!"

"But Owl," said Pinwheel.

"I need to stay in bed. I am trying to

have my best dream ever."

"Nonsense," said Owl.

"You can dream at night."

Pinwheel pulled the covers right
over his head.
He closed his eyes.

He tossed. He turned.

At last he fell asleep.

He had a dream.

In this dream, he was in a field.

There were flowers everywhere.

Squirrel and Rabbit and Owl
were there.
They all played hide-and-seek.
Then Rabbit gave them each a muffin.
It was the best muffin Pinwheel had
ever tasted.

When Pinwheel woke up,
he was smiling.
"That was a wonderful dream!"
he said.
"I can't wait to tell Squirrel and Owl
and Rabbit all about it."

He jumped out of bed and
ran outside.

"Squirrel! Owl! Rabbit!" he called.

"Where are you? It's me, Pinwheel!

I am awake. I am up. I am back."

But no one answered.

"Squirrel!" he called.

"Are you still hiding?

Rabbit, are you eating muffins?

Owl, there <u>are</u> colors everywhere!"

But nobody answered.

Where were his friends?

He ran into the field.

His friends were playing hide-and-seek.

"Good morning!" he called.

"Good afternoon," they answered.

"Did you have your most wonderful dream ever?" asked Squirrel.

"Yes, I did!" said Pinwheel.

"Tell us about it," said Owl.

Pinwheel looked at the flowers.

Then he remembered his dream.

"My dream was wonderful," he said.

"But now that I am with my friends,

I am going to have my most

wonderful day ever.

And that is even better!"